Two n
side of th

A sig

MOOS
CROSSIN

Books in the Moose and Hildy series

Moose and Hildy

Moose Crossing

by **Stephanie Greene**
illustrated by **Joe Mathieu**

Marshall Cavendish Children

Text copyright © 2005 by Stephanie Greene
Illustrations copyright © 2005 by Marshall Cavendish
First Marshall Cavendish paperback edition, 2010

Marshall Cavendish Corporation
99 White Plains Road, Tarrytown, NY 10591
www.marshallcavendish.us/kids

Library of Congress Cataloging-in-Publication Data
Greene, Stephanie.
Moose crossing / by Stephanie Greene ; illustrated by Joe Mathieu.
p. cm. — (Moose and Hildy)
Summary: Moose is excited when the sign "Moose Crossing" is put up,
but he finds that tourists and fans can be exhausting.
ISBN 0-7614-5233-8 (hardcover) 978-0-7614-5699-5 (paperback)
[1. Moose—Fiction. 2. Fame—Fiction.] I. Mathieu, Joseph, ill. II. Title
III. Series: Greene, Stephanie. Moose and Hildy.
PZ7.G8434Mn 2005
[E]—dc22
2004027577

The illustrations were created with Prismacolor pencil
and Dr. Martin gray wash.

A Marshall Cavendish Chapter Book
Book design by Adam Mietlowski

Printed in China (E)
1 3 5 6 4 2

Marshall Cavendish
Children

To Oliver and George, two stars
—S.G.

Lovingly dedicated to my mother, Patricia Mathieu
—J.M.

Contents

Chapter One

Moose's Own Sign

Moose was getting out of the tub when he heard the noise.

He grabbed his binoculars and ran to the window.

Two men were putting up a sign by the side of the road. One man pounded a metal pole into the ground.

The other man put the sign on it.

Then they got back into their truck and drove away.

A sign? thought Moose. What do we need a sign for? Nothing ever happens around here.

He ran through the woods to see what it said.

"Moose Crossing," he read.

"Oh, my," said Moose. "My own sign."

They were two of the most beautiful words he'd ever seen.

"Dear Mom" didn't come close.

"Oh, my," he said again. "I must be very important to have my own sign."

The more he thought about it, the more important Moose felt.

People must have noticed his antlers. They had fallen off again, the way they did every fall.

But they'd grow back, more magnificent than ever.

Or maybe they had noticed his legs.

Moose looked down. So what if his knees knocked? Those little bumps on his calves were sheer muscle.

Moose strutted to the other side of the road.

He turned around and strutted back.

He struck a pose.

Imagine. His own sign.

People would come from miles around to take his picture. They'd stand in line for his autograph.

This was the most exciting thing that had ever happened to him. Moose could hardly wait to tell his friends.

He didn't have to wait long.

"Hi, Moose," called a cheerful voice. "Are you ready to go?"

Chapter Two

A Falling Out

It was Hildy, his best friend.

"You won't believe it!" called Moose. "Come see!"

"Moose Crossing," read Hildy. "Where did this come from?"

"Two men put it up this morning," said Moose. "I guess people have been talking about me."

"It's very nice," said Hildy. "Come on. Let's go swimming."

"I can't leave *now*," said Moose.

"Why not?"

"I have to watch my sign."

"Watch it do what?" asked Hildy. "It's just a sign."

"I wouldn't call it *just* a sign," Moose said with a sniff. "I think I might read it for a while."

"Read it? It has only two words."

"I know," said Moose. "Aren't they beautiful?"

"Oh, Moose." Hildy laughed. "You're so ridiculous."

"Ridiculous?" Moose frowned. "Do you think people would have made me my own sign if they thought I was ridiculous?"

"It's not *your* sign, you silly thing."

"Oh. So, now I'm silly."

"Moose, stop joking." Hildy looked at him closely. "You *are* joking, aren't you?"

Moose turned his head away.

"It's not your sign," Hildy said gently. "It's for all the moose around here."

"I see. All the moose."

Moose looked to the left. He looked to the right.

He shielded his eyes from the sun and squinted into the distance. "I don't see any other moose around here, do you, Hildy?"

"Moose!" Hildy stamped her foot. "What's gotten into you?"

"You know what I think?" said Moose. "I think you're jealous."

"Jealous! Of what?"

"That you're not special enough to have your own sign."

"Well, I never!" Now it was Hildy's turn to sound mad. "I may not be *special enough*, as you say. But at least I don't have a swelled head, like *some* folks I know."

"Sticks and stones might break my bones, but names will never hurt me," said Moose.

"Fine. You probably shouldn't go swimming anyway. With a head as fat as yours, you'd probably sink."

Hildy stomped off.

"Call me when the swelling goes down!" she shouted.

Moose was too busy admiring his sign to hear.

The closer he got, the better it looked.

But wait. Was that a scratch?

Tsk, tsk. A brand-new sign and it already had a scratch.

He'd have to get his furniture polish and a rag. Maybe some silver polish for the pole.

Moose's head was full of plans as he hurried home. He had a lot to do before his fans arrived.

For arrive they would.

Moose could hardly wait.

Chapter Three

Fans, at Last

The first car arrived while Moose was eating lunch.

A man with a camera got out of the front seat. He waved his arms around like a policeman directing traffic. A woman and little boy went and stood on either side of the sign.

The man took their picture.

"Oh, my," said Moose. "Fans."

Moose put his dishes in the dishwasher. By the time he looked again, there were three more cars, two campers, and a motorcycle.

"Oh, my," Moose said again. He felt a funny flutter in his stomach.

17

How should he act, now that he was famous?

He looked in the mirror.

Humble yet proud?

Moose pointed his nose in the air and smiled.

What about shy but interested?

Moose looked down, then peered up through his eyelashes.

Humble but proud, he decided. That was the best.

Moose checked to see if there was food between his teeth. He grabbed his favorite pen. Then he took a deep breath and opened the door.

The crowd was making so much noise, no one heard him coming. When Moose stepped out from behind a tree, there was a shocked silence.

Then the little boy shouted, "Look, Ma! It's a moose!"

"Good heavens," said a woman. "Would you get a load of that nose?"

"What about those legs?" said a man.

Moose smiled modestly.

"Everyone stand back!" ordered the man with the camera. "It might charge."

Charge? thought Moose. I wouldn't dream of charging. Free autographs for the crowd!

20

He reached for his pen.

"Look out!" called a voice. "It has a weapon!"

"Quick!" yelled another voice. "Get its picture!"

People started to shout. Babies started to cry. Flashbulbs started popping like it was the Fourth of July.

Moose turned on his heels and ran.

Chapter Four

Being Held Prisoner

More fans arrived the next day.

And the next.

At night, Moose lay in his bed and listened to radios blaring and dogs barking.

In the morning, he woke up hoping they'd be gone.

It only got worse.

People pitched tents and set up lawn chairs. There was a volleyball net, an ice-cream stand, and a man selling hot dogs.

Someone had moose T-shirts for sale.

Moose longed to talk to Hildy. But he was too proud to call.

On the third day he was sitting in his living room, feeling sorry for himself, when the phone rang.

"Hello?"

"Oh, Moose," said Hildy. "I'm sorry we argued. Will you forgive me?"

"Will you forgive *me*?"

"I already have," said Hildy.

"Me, too," said Moose.

"Oh, goody, we're best friends again. I'll be right over."

"No, don't!" cried Moose. "It's too dangerous."

"What do you mean?"

"I'm being held prisoner," said Moose.

"You are?"

"I'm afraid so." Moose sighed. "A prisoner of my own conceit."

"Oh, Moose. You had me scared for a minute."

"But it's true," said Moose. "I wanted fans and I got them. Now I can't get rid of them."

He told Hildy everything.

"Poor Moose," she said. "What are you going to do?"

"What else can I do? I have to come up with a plan."

"Can I help?"

"Thanks, Hildy," said Moose, "but I got myself into this. It's up to me to get myself out."

Chapter Five

Moose's Plan

"Tallyho!" called Moose as he dashed into the clearing.

"Look!" shouted a little boy. "It's a —" He stopped. "Say, what are you, anyway?"

"Why, I'm a horse, of course," said Moose. "Come on! Let's go to the races!"

"We're waiting to see a moose," said a man.

"Moose are boring," said Moose. "Have you ever heard of anyone playing a game of moose-shoes?"

"We drove all the way from Florida," said a woman.

"Or going moose-back riding?" Moose chuckled. "Of course not."

"I want to see a moose!" yelled the little boy.

"Well, you won't see any around here," said Moose.

"What about that sign?" said a woman.

"That old thing?"

"It looks brand-new."

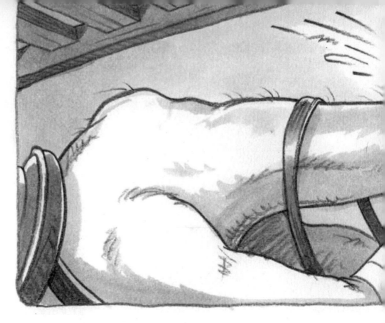

"She's right," said another woman. "Someone's been polishing it."

"Yeah, and these people saw one the other day, but he ran away."

"You won't see him again," Moose said quickly. "He's gone."

"How do you know?"

"He left on the train I came in on."

"Aw, this guy's crazy," said the man with the camera. "Whoever heard of a moose taking a train?"

"Yeah," said the little boy. "He's just a jealous old horse."

Old? thought Moose.

He ran home and stood in front of the mirror. The boy was right. There were two fine lines between his eyes.

Stress lines. They had to be.

Moose fell onto his couch with a groan.

His fans were going to be the death of him.

At the rate he was aging, he wouldn't even be around for the funeral.

Chapter Six

Moose Mumps

"Rex Sneed, *The Daily News*," said Moose. He pulled the brim of his fedora down over his sunglasses and the collar of his trench coat up over his nose.

"What's a newspaper reporter doing in the woods?" said a woman.

"Covering the outbreak," said Moose.

"What outbreak?" said a man.

"Moose mumps."

"Moose mumps?" The man with the camera sounded suspicious. "What's that?"

"You know that growth at the end of a moose's nose?" said Moose. "Looks like a baked potato?"

Heads nodded.

"That's moose mumps," said Moose. "First, the nose swells. Then it turns purple. In bad cases, it falls off."

"My goodness," said a woman. "Is it contagious?"

"Worse than chicken pox," Moose said. "I'd advise you folks to get as far away from here as possible. And fast."

People started to run. Then a shrill voice shouted, "Hey! Aren't you that horse that was here yesterday?"

Everyone stopped.

"You are," said the little boy, scowling up at Moose. "You're that crazy horse."

"What makes you say that?" said Moose.

"You've got the same lines between your eyes."

"The kid's right," said a man. "They look like railroad tracks."

"Wait!" cried Moose. "I can explain . . ."

But nobody wanted to listen.

Moose gave up and went home.

Chapter Seven

His Last Hope

The phone was ringing when Moose opened his front door.

"Are they gone?" Hildy asked.

"No." Moose slumped into a chair.

"What are you going to do now?"

"The only thing I *can* do," said Moose. "I have to go away."

"Go away?" said Hildy. "For how long?"

"Two years . . . maybe three."

"It's all because of that silly sign!" said Hildy. "I'd like to come over there and chop it down."

"They'd just put you in jail," Moose said glumly. "Then we'd both be prisoners."

41

"Oh, Moose. I wish there was something I could do."

Moose sat up. "I think you just did."

"I did?" said Hildy. "How?"

"You gave me a great idea," said Moose. "I've got to go, Hildy. There isn't a minute to lose."

"Okay, but I'm coming over there tomorrow, no matter what."

Moose hung up and went in search of a piece of cardboard.

It was a long shot, but it might work.

And it was the only shot Moose had left.

Chapter Eight

Midnight Maneuvers

When the alarm woke Moose up at midnight, it was raining.

Good, he thought. That means no moon.

He put on his favorite shaggy-dog slippers. He threw his comforter over his head. Then he walked quickly through the woods until he came to the clearing.

There wasn't a sound.

Moose tiptoed past the tents and the campers and the shuttered hot dog stand until he came to the sign. He took out the cardboard and taped it to the pole.

Then he headed home.

He was almost past the last tent when the sleepy voice of a little boy said, "What's that?"

Moose froze.

"What's what?" It was a woman's voice.

"That noise."

"I didn't hear anything."

"It sounded like Grandma in those dumb slippers Dad gave her for Christmas."

"Go to sleep," said the woman. "It's the middle of the night."

Moose stayed as still as a statue.

Five minutes passed.

Ten.

There were no sounds from inside the tent.

Moose tiptoed into the woods and broke into a run. He locked his front door, jumped into bed, and pulled his covers over his head.

All he could do was wait for morning.

Only then would he know if his plan had worked.

Chapter Nine

Free, at Last!

"Moose!" shouted Hildy. "Are you all right?"

She ran into the clearing and screeched to a stop. "What a mess," she said.

The garbage cans were overflowing. The grass had been trampled to mud. Soda cans and plastic bottles and food wrappers were everywhere.

But not a single fan.

"I know," said Moose. "Isn't it wonderful?"

"Where is everyone?"

"Gone." Moose stabbed a candy wrapper with his stick and dropped it into the bag around his neck. "They cleared out first thing this morning."

"How'd you do it?" asked Hildy.

"Remember when you said you wanted to chop down the sign?"

Hildy nodded.

"It made me think," said Moose. "The pen's mightier than the sword, isn't it?"

"That's what they say," said Hildy.

"Well, this proves it." Moose led her over to the sign. "Look."

Underneath the old sign was a new sign:

20 MILES AHEAD

"Moose!" Hildy cried. "You're a genius!"

"Careful," said Moose. "You don't want me getting a swelled head again."

Hildy's laugh was interrupted by an unmistakable sound.

"Quick! They're back!" cried Moose.

Hildy and Moose dove behind a bush. A car sped around the corner and came to

a halt. A woman rolled down the front window.

"Twenty miles ahead," she read.

"Twenty miles?" wailed a voice from the backseat. "I'm sick of driving."

"Me, too," came another wail. "Who cares about a dumb old moose?"

The car took off in a cloud of dust.

"Did you hear that?" said Moose.

"It didn't hurt your feelings, did it?" said Hildy.

"Are you kidding?" Moose stood up and dusted off his knees. "The more people who don't want to see a dumb old moose, the better. Come on, Hildy. Let's go swimming."